# EVERY DAY WAS THE SAME.

Like always, the jangling bell rang and rang. Mauk's

there in the morning," Mauk said. The world was so new and wonderful, it was hard

to believe he had once thought that

tired. He climbed into bed and dropped his boots on the floor. "I hope they're still

boots were on the ceiling. And once more he was late for the Master. ∞ Mauk was ☞

water and fish swam in the sky! He raced home through the dark. ∞ Mauk was

helping the Master build a grand *Palazzo.* “What does he want now?” Mauk

seemed strange and mysterious as he ran across the bridge. Birds flew through the

wondered as he ran. He had already sharpened the Master's pencils. ∞ The palace

could not tell which was the palace and which the reflection. ∞ Everything

floated in the middle of the lake. It looked almost like the Master's drawing,

looked out over the water. The *Palazzo*, floating on the lake, was perfect. Mauk

Mauk thought. But something about the towers did not seem quite right. ∞ He

from the tower. Then everything went quiet. The lake was hushed. ∞ Mauk

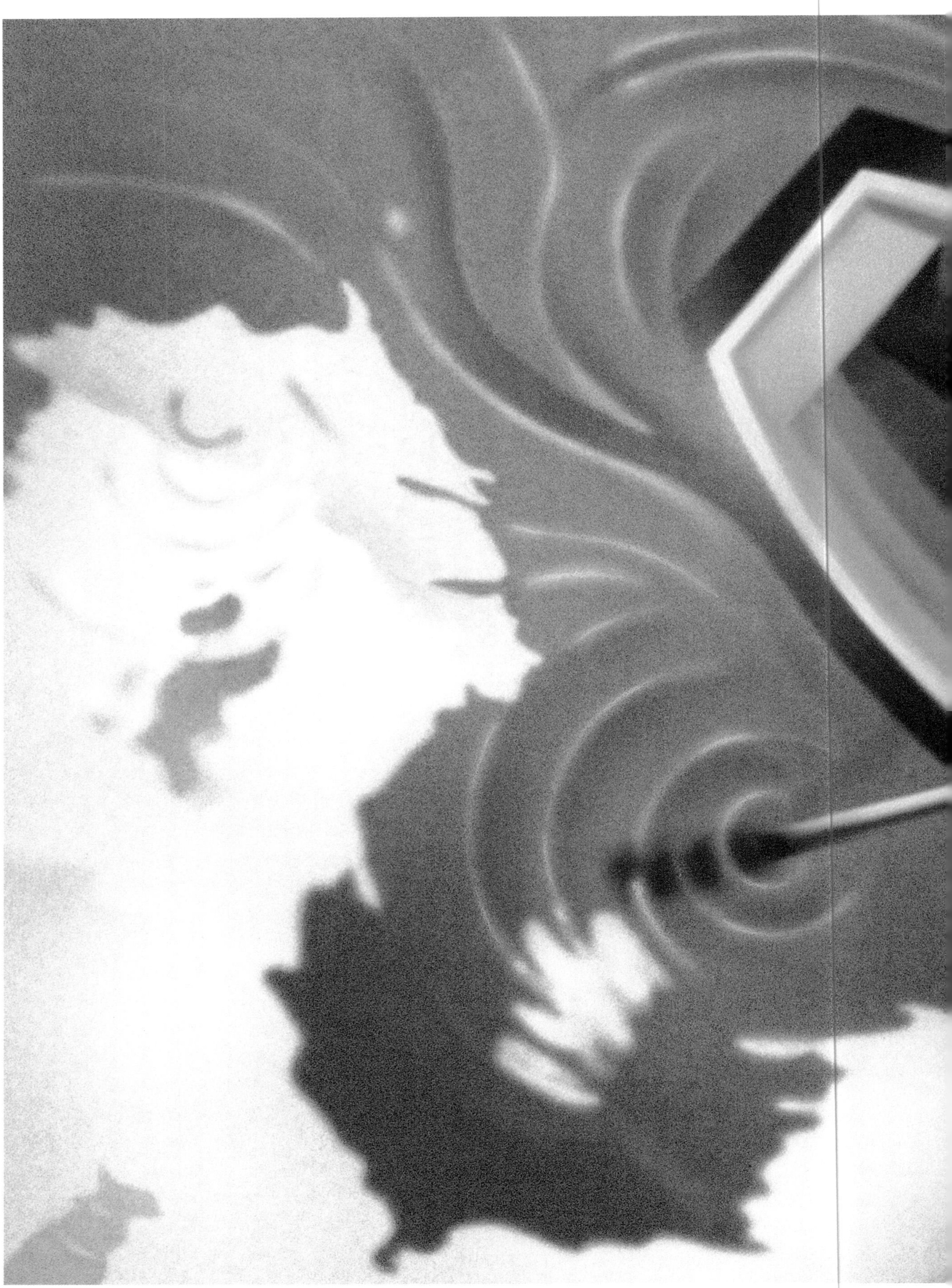

paddled across the lake, just as he did every day when the Master called. But today

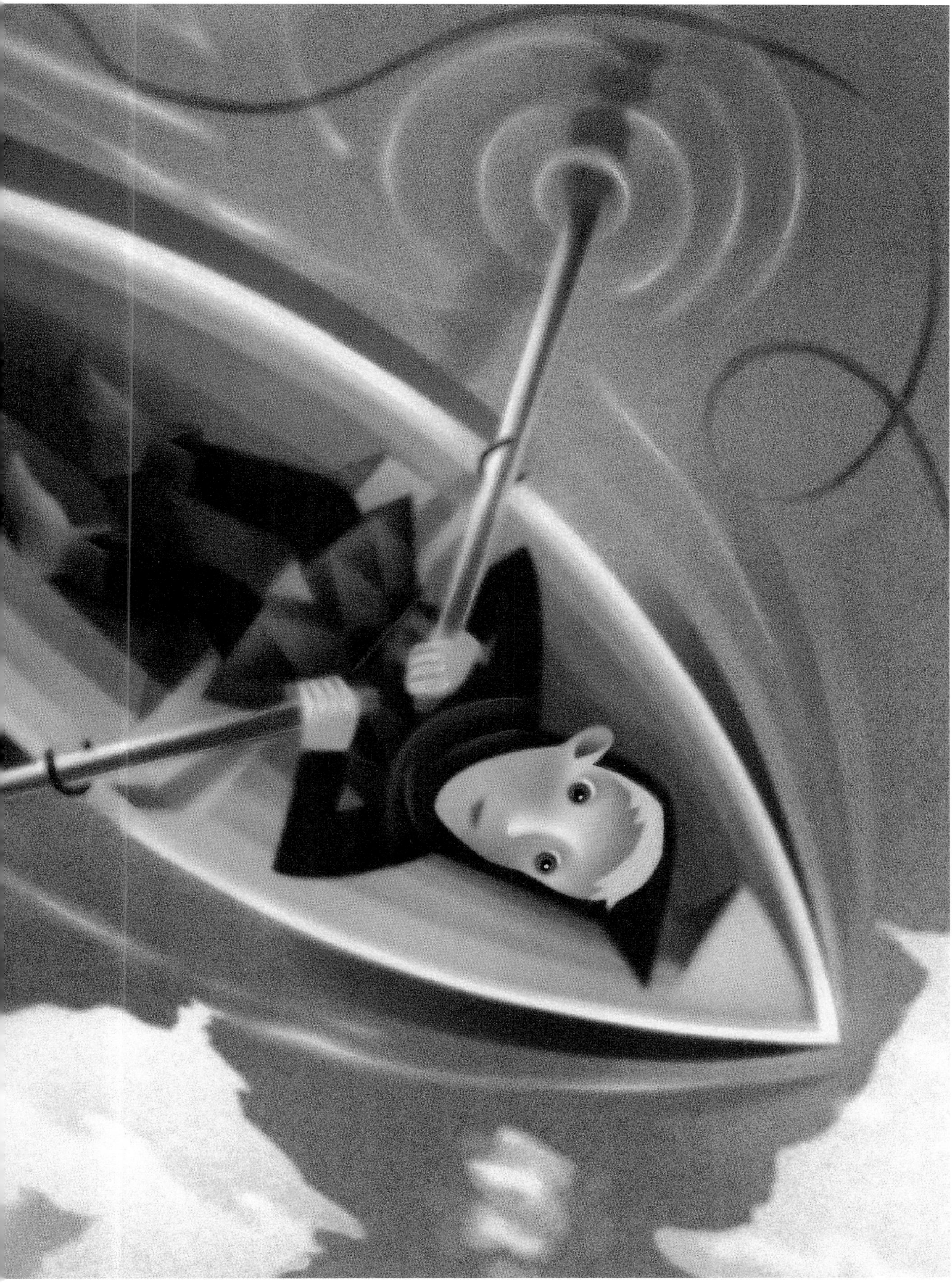

the *Palazzo* seemed different. ∞ How strange it looked, shimmering in the

fading light. The *Palazzo* was dark. Mauk could still hear the workers calling

*Palazzo Inverso!* "It *is* beautiful," he thought. ∞ And he paddled away in the

morning mist. ∞ Mauk skipped up the steps to the grand entry. The doorway to the

spun out the door and cartwheeled down the steps. Everyone loved Mauk's

*Palazzo* was right where he would have drawn it, if only the Master had—even once!—

at all. They were cheering him on! Mauk saw that even the Master was smiling. ∞ He

let Mauk draw. ∞ Inside, the painters painted and the carpenters hammered

and sawed. Workers wheeled their carts in all directions. ∞ Mauk wondered why

the workers were after him. He stopped to look back. They were not chasing him

He knew that the underside of the stairs was the fastest way out. ∞ Mauk thought

the palace looked so strange. What was different? It was not the stairs.

every inch of the upside-down *Palazzo*. He knew every doorway and every window.

He counted them as he ran down to the tower. ∞ The workers had made

he jumped over the bricklayers' cart and raced on. ∞ Only Mauk knew

the right number of steps. Did he forget to order bricks? No, here were the

every hallway and every secret passage. "Watch out above you!" he called as

bricklayers with a full cart—spilling bricks on the ceiling! ∞ Mauk ran through the workers without touching the floor. ∞ Mauk knew every staircase. He knew

every room in the *Palazzo*. Finally he could see what was wrong. All around him,

workers were falling down stairs, hanging from windows, and shouting. ∞ Even the

painters were shouting Mauk's name, but that did not stop him. He whirled past and laughed. "Race you to the chandelier!" he called. ∞ From below, the

Mistress was snapping at the Master. "You're tracking mud on the wall," she cried.

"Well, you're standing on the ceiling!" the Master answered. ∞ The *Palazzo* was all

upside down. Mauk turned here and turned there. He dashed past the carpenters

upside down was that now Mauk could run on the ceiling! ∞ He *liked* being

mixed up. Workers were walking on their hands down the stairs! The water

Mauk. But no one could catch him. The best thing about turning the drawing

in the fountain was falling up instead of down. ∞ Everyone was blaming

trickster!" the Master called. ∞ The workers ran in circles and pointed up at

the Master. "This tower is upside down!" the Mistress said. "No, it's downside

on the ladder. He slid down headfirst before anyone could catch him. "Catch the

*up!*" the Master cried. ∞ "Let's all look at the drawing," Mauk said, climbing

“Don’t let him get away!” the Mistress called. ∞ But Mauk was already

in the window. “You changed my *Palazzo!*” the Master shouted, pointing at Mauk.

spun away to the window. “You’ve ruined my beautiful *Palazzo!*” the Master cried.

“But I didn’t draw anything!” Mauk said. He was not allowed to draw. ∞ Mauk

"it looks even better like this!" Mauk said, standing on his head. Then he

only sharpened the Master's pencils—except when the Master was looking out

the window. Then Mauk might have turned the drawing around just a tiny bit this way. What difference would that make? Sometimes the Master's nap gave Mauk the chance to turn the picture a bit more this way. So the Master never noticed what a strange *Palazzo* he was drawing! "But

# AUTHOR'S NOTE

The apprentice Mauk is an entirely fictional character who takes his nickname and his inspiration from the work of the Dutch artist M. C. Escher (1898–1972).

Maurits Cornelis Escher was the talented son of a civil engineer and, before the age of thirteen, learned carpentry and developed his gift for drawing. As a young man he briefly studied architecture at the Haarlem School for Architecture and Decorative Arts, but with the encouragement of one of his teachers soon changed direction. He would study art and design.

Escher made the right choice. As an artist, he was free to draw believable-looking buildings that could not be built. Escher's skill at playing with perspective and tricking people into seeing his version of three-dimensional space made him world famous.

In a work called "Ascending and Descending," Escher drew stairs that lead down and around a building's inner courtyard yet appear to go back and end where they began. These endless loops going nowhere became his trademark. He realized that with a few carefully drawn steps he could take a person out of the real world and into his world of the impossible.



Houghton Mifflin Books for Children is an imprint of Houghton Mifflin Harcourt Publishing Company.

www.hmhbooks.com

The text of this book is set in Bodoni Seventy Two ITC Std
The illustrations are mixed media.

Library of Congress Cataloging-in-Publication Data is on file.
ISBN 978-0-547-23999-6

Printed in Singapore
TWP 10 9 8 7 6 5 4 3 2 1